FINDING
ISAIAH

A SHORT STORY BY FELICIA GUY-LYNCH

Dedication

To all those striving
to maintain salvation

FINDING ISAIAH

Praise for *Finding Isaiah*

"This story started off unlike the usual and ended the same. The usual would be to start off shitty and have a happy ending. The story started off as a family's dream but as life happened in the story, things changed and left us, the readers, captivated and curious to know how things will end and if things will get better for this family. It was a roller-coaster read. Fluctuating scenes took me through an emotional toll but kept me reading. A great story, great lessons, and strong characters, with a lovely twist to a happy ending."

- Aziza Brown

"Finding Isaiah," offers strong life lessons that can help one avoid taking the wrong path. This short story has a worthy plot intertwined with nuggets of wisdom and wrapped in a tale of pain, struggle and hardship that many of us can connect with and relate to. This story will have you both smirking and frowning at innumerable points in the story."

- Candace Shepherd

"If you're an adult, as old as I am or maybe older; when reading that story, you will be transported back to your childhood. If you're younger, you'll be able to identify with various situations that this young man faces. FINDING ISAIAH is this coming-of-age story that gives you a break from your reality and allows you to enter a new one. She is one of the most talented women I have had the chance to encounter. To not only take on a series of novels, but to take on this particular project and do it in the voice of a young man at that says a lot about her as a writer."

- Robert Mulolo

"She has outdone herself with this promising series. It executes the journey through urban fiction in the heart of Toronto with the phenomenal and gut-wrenching adventures evident in the "Finding Isaiah"
series. Get ready to be blown away by the experiences Is aiah must overcome to become who he is destined to be"

- Khadijah Powell-Kelly

"She writes from a woman's view, which is subtly evident by the underlying sensitivity of the main characters, while still understanding and evoking male strength. In addition, there is a beautiful naivety in Isaiah's words about the sanctity of marriage and commitment. The idealism of a woman, as heard through Isaiah's voice, is humbling in a world of bravado and constant indecency. The message that one should never conform and always look to become a leader is evident and powerful throughout the story."

- Waleed Elabed

Preface

They say you don't truly know a man unless you walk in his shoes. Although I'm writing from a woman's perspective, women and men have the same desire. That desire is to love and be loved. This is why I challenged myself to write this book.

The purpose of writing this book is to write from a perspective outside of my own. The basis of this publication come from discussions I had with people of all walk of life (especially men). Framing the premise and the structure for the story was not as difficult as I anticipated. I had a lot of fun extrapolating different storylines and creating an original one.

I chose to write from my interpretations of a man's perspective in an attempt to see life through the lens of the opposite sex. 'Finding Isaiah' will surprise you, build up anticipation within you and make you fall in love with the journey of the experience.

Without further ado, I am most humbled to disseminate, 'Finding Isaiah' into your hands. May your mind receive edification while reading just as much as I learned while writing it.

Sincerely,

Felicia Guy-Lynch

Chapter 1

I am a 1990's, Scarborough-born baby. Mom named me Isaiah. She was nineteen when she had me. They say she had the brightest glow when she was carrying me. Her countenance was full of class. She worked as a nurse, healing people back to health. Dad, like any man, was proud of having me as his new baby boy

In fact, they were high school sweethearts. They loved each other dearly.

We lived in a residential area. Our house was decent: cherry wood floors, one-of-a-kind furniture and the latest Apple products.

I'm thankful I had a father growing up. He was a very hardworking man, a force to reckon with and a philosopher in his own right. His presence was very necessary because only a man can teach me how to be a man. He didn't speak much but when he did, he had something deep to say. Actions speak volumes. Intentions tune them.

Dad's zeal for cars was enormous. He obtained his apprenticeship in Auto Mechanics at Centennial College. He was the first of his friends to get his driver's license. His first job was at *Splash N Shine Hand Car Wash Detailing.* He saved up and bought his first car. It was a red 1987 Acura Integra. Eventually, he left his job to own his own garage. He also owned his own car garage. He named it *Metal Chariot Shop.*

He would tell me he was never too big on working for people. It was just a stepping stone to get where he wanted to be. He was well respected for being honest and reasonable as a Car Technician. If you needed to get your car serviced, Dad was the man.

He taught me the importance of being my own man. Followers are easily led astray. Failure only comes when I quit. If I mess up, I should learn from my mistakes and try again: I've got nothing to lose. See value in the intangible: material possession, like the body, are transitory. Family first. Protect the clan. Be mindful of the little things: in the long run, they make a big difference. Leave work's stress at *work*. Lead with a sound mind. All the answers we're looking for are inside. We all have the Most High in us. *Never* forget to pay homage to the Most High in all of us. Be your own best friend more. If I was going to make love to a woman, I needed to wrap it up. My wet dreams are going to come to life one way or another. A man is just a man. Good things come to those who wait. Sometimes, better things come to those who go after it. Have a plan then execute to get what you want.

The first time he took me to Scarborough Bluffs, I was ten years old. The waves of the shore made me feel less edgy. It was here he taught me the importance of silence. "In the midst of chaos," he said, "keep stillness within. The only real battle is with yourself. Fight to keep your peace. Nobody else can do that for you. There's also something about being by a body of water that clears the mind. Makes it easier to prioritize. Nature always heals. Our bodies are made up of all the elements we see around us. If we need healing of the mind, we like the shore, should study the turbulence within and create a calm as we see fit."

Even Mom showed me a thing or two. She told me it's important to sow my seed on fertile ground. The ground was a woman's womb. No toxic ground ever produced fruitfully.

My parents encouraged me to look after my brother, do well in school and stay busy with extracurricular. Jafari was growing up too. He was thirteen. Unlike most younger brothers, he actually listens to me when I talk. I couldn't ask for more.

In school, I was an A student. Gifted program. Love to read. The World's Biggest Bookstore was my intellectual sanctuary.

In between reading, I played chess. I sure as hell am not a pawn. I love those positions to millions. Minions don't even know they're pawns. They think it's checkers. It's chess, *never* checkers. Their ignorance can be forgiven but ignorance can only go on for so long. We live in the age of information. After a while, there are no excuses for not knowing what's *really* going on. Everyone grows at their own pace.

Fall 2008, I met this beauty in science class. Her name's Naomi. Five, five with brown eyes. Like the "Girl Next Door." She dressed in a lot of floral clothing. Bright colours. Her legs looked lovely in those floral dresses. And her feet were small and cute. My eyes would fluctuate easily in and out of her pretty frame.

She was always participating in class. Very smart. She was always smiling and made the class laugh from time to time. A girl with wits and humour is always refreshing. I'll make my move when the time's right.

Chapter 2

Haze was my right-hand man. A brother from another mother. We stayed out of trouble and kept to ourselves like Beavis and Buthead (only thing is we actually had our head on right).

As much as Dad taught me to have a strong mind, he also emphasized the importance of having a healthy body. So, I practised Taekwondo.

After practise, I would have out with Haze. He lived in Malvern. We were both eighteen. We met each other on the first day of orientation 5 years ago.

We practised together on Tuesdays to Thursdays at the John Lau International School of Taekwondo. Our teacher's name was Jeonsa. He taught like a warrior because I felt like one after his classes. He was strict but fair. Classes got smaller week by week. He said those who stuck it out were the warriors he was meant to train. What I appreciated about him was his no-nonsense approach to how he taught. He always taught us that it was more important to establish mental strength. If you lack it, you were twice defeated, making your training null and void.

Chapter 3

Saturday evening, a quarter after seven. Almost six hours after Dad's rant. He was upset about a worker not coming and not calling in advance. It was his day off and he was looking forward to just relaxing. When things don't go as planned, he had to pay the cost to be the boss. It was too vivid to forget. That's when my cell rang. "Isaiah. I'm coming to pick you up." I didn't recognize the soft voice.

"Who is this?" I asked.

"This is Naomi. Mom asked me to pick you up and bring you over here."

"Oh. I didn't know you had such as close relationship with Mom."

"I know," she said. "I'll be there in a half an hour."

After she hung up the phone, I called the Humber River Region Hospital to see if Mom was still working but they told me she left for the day. I wish I could call her directly but she didn't have a cell phone. Something felt off.

I wanted to know what was going on because it felt like the longest half hour of my life.

She finally arrived. "What's going on?" I asked. I was feeling anxious.

"I'll tell you when we get there."

We pulled up at Lawrence Avenue East and Mc-Cowan Road, close to the Scarborough Hospital. I felt uneasy. After parking the car, she rested her hand on my hand and looked me in the eyes, teary, "Your father is in the hospital. He's been stabbed and robbed."

I saw red. I was dumbfounded. I was in denial for a split second. My mind was completely devoid of thought. My heart felt like it stopped beating for a minute. I felt stagnant. What am I going to do now?

"He got stabbed in the gut. I don't know how he is. Your Mom is upstairs with him right now. Go check on how your father is doing."

"Come with me," I pleaded.

She agreed and parked across the hospital because she wanted to avoid having to pay for parking.

Mom looked so broken when I glimpsed in her direction. Her face was full of tears. When she looked at me and all I could see was her in despair. She hugged me and I hugged her back firmly. While holding her, she sobbed, "I wish I stopped him from leaving."

"Mom. Now isn't the time to beat yourself up. Do you know what happened? Will he be ok?"

"He's going to be just fine. They're doing surgery on him right now," she said, still sobbing. "I should have just stopped him from going through that door," she murmured. "I should have calmed him down. I never should have-"

"What happened?" I asked once again.

"I never should have let him out the door upset. I should have said something! If only I'd known! That coward will get what's rightfully his. I will leave him to time." She rubbed one side of my face. "Your father is in good hands," she said trying to be reassuring. "You take Jafari and stay with Naomi."

"Where are you going, Mom? Can I see Dad?"

She didn't answer and made an exit out of the waiting room.

I was being held back by the doctors and nurses. I really wanted to see my father. They kept informing me, "He's on the operating table and will be transferred to intensive care afterwards."

My mind calmed down as I sat around waiting. I called Haze. "I have no idea who did this to my father. At the same time, nothing goes unpunished." He did his best to uplift me in these hard times.

"Where are you now?" Haze asked.

"The Scarborough Hospital," I barely spoke.

"Where's Jafari?"

"At the Scarborough Village Recreation Centre."

"Naomi. Is she there?" he was very curious. "I'm glad you have her as a part of your support system."

"Me too. I'll call you later on with updates."

"Ok. Stay strong."

Naomi and I left the hospital to go pick up Jafari. After picking him up, we drove back to my house. Mom was standing on the front porch. Waiting. Her purple dress exudes royalty. Her hands were rubbing her arms. She embraced Naomi as if she were her daughter. She hugged all of us so warm and gentle. The house was very clean. John Lennon's *Imagine* was playing in the background. Mom took Naomi into the guest room. Naomi came out not too long after, gently saying good night as she left the house.

Mom followed me into my bedroom. I said nothing. Mom looked more hopeful than the time I saw her. I switched the light on in my room.

"Ok, Mom. Let me know what's going on. How's Dad?" I asked.

"Your father is doing alright. He's a fighter. He'll be home in a week and a half. He'll have bandages. he's going to have to relax for a while. We will help him kale it more tolerable. You know how prideful he can get," she added, "he will have to get his stitches treated after a couple of weeks."

We sat for a moment in silence, still taking in the situation. A moment of silence manifested. I spoke my mind. "When Naomi called and said she was coming to pick us up, I wish I was able to reach you right there and then."

"It's good you wanted to confirm," Mom said. "Naomi can be trusted. She's like my daughter. Everything was fine. Right?"

"Yes. Everything was good. She was very pleasant and supportive. Where did you meet Naomi?"

"She volunteers at the hospital I work at. She's finishing up the last of her community hours. She's very eager to work. I took a liking to her. I would take breaks at the same time as her and she was very friendly. We talked about all sorts of things. Her focus at such a young age is very admirable. Her parents died in a car accident two years ago and she's been staying with her Mom's side of the family. So, I adopted her as my daughter. I wanted to show her that people still care for orphans like herself."

"Sorry to hear about her parents. I'm glad you took her under your wing. She's also in my science class."

"Yes. I know. She told me. I want you to meet and settle down with a nice girl like Naomi."

I smiled. Mom has good taste.

Chapter 4

Two weeks went by after the stabbing. It was different not having Dad around. It's not something I wanted to get used to either. When Dad arrived home, the look of sadness on Jafari's face was hard to ignore. Dad was slimmer than before. The bruise on his head was healing.

Later on, that day, while Mom was out, I pushed Dad's door open and went in. "Hey, Dad. Are you feeling better?" He answered but his words were inaudible. "Ok, Dad. It's alright," I said, smiling to make him feel better. He managed to crack half a smile.

When I got home after practise, I noticed Mom's Mazda was nowhere in sight. I got inside and Dad called out my name. "Why are you still up?" I asked.

"They took the car. They took your Mom."

"Who took Mom?"

"The police. They had a warrant out for her arrest for fraud. Jafari was beside himself. Your mother was crying and told me how sorry she was while they arrested her. I told her it's ok. We will do our best to get her out. I'm tired."

"I don't know what to say," I said. Unbelievable. Mom and fraud? It doesn't sound good together.

We both knocked out. The next morning, Dad contacted Mom's lawyer. The lawyer told Dad to come to his office Tuesday. I stayed back to catch up on some sleep.

Now that Mom's gone, how are we going to survive? Why would she commit fraud? Was she running out of savings because Dad's been off of work for a while? Why do things like this keep happening?

Tuesday morning came but the alarm didn't go off. Dad was so tired he set the alarm to 7pm instead of 7am. I woke up Dad and told him to call the lawyer because we woke up too late to meet Mom at the courthouse. He left a message.

We got hit with reality. The reality of having to downsize. Selling the house was our best bet. I grew up all my life in this house. I surely was going to miss it.

I found Dad drinking Grey Goose. I removed the bottle from his mouth.

"Is this going to solve our problems?" I asked. He broke down.

"All our hard work is going down the drain! We were well off. I had a successful business running and your Mom had a good job as a nurse. I can't understand why she would do something like this behind my back and commit fraud with Oliver. That man's always been jealous of me. We fought over Mom back in high school. He was making her feel uncomfortable. Before that, Oliver and I were the best of friends. It's so funny how after all these years, your once-best friend can turn into your biggest arch-nemesis. I feel betrayed by your mother. She knows how I feel about him. How dare she!"

"We don't know why but we will see her tomorrow and ask her all the questions we want answers to."

Bright and early the next morning, we arrived at the courthouse.

"The judge has granted bail for $50,000. In the meantime, you can visit her at the Toronto East Detention Centre," said her lawyer.

Dad and I sighed in relief. We were relieved that she was able to at least make bail. What was in our favour was we had a good amount of equity in the house. We could use the proceeds from selling the house today of Mom's bail from the line of credit. We were also looking forward to seeing her tomorrow.

By Wednesday, Dad was ready to go see Mom. She walked into the room with an officer by her side. I smiled and she smiled back. "How are you guys?" She asked.

"We're hanging in there." I replied.

"Yea. I miss you guys."

Dad budded in, "I'm going to sell the house to make up for the rest of your bond."

"Alright. You guys pray for me. I'm so sorry," she broke down. I was going to ask her why she got charged with fraud but I didn't want to interrogate her under these circumstances.

Chapter 5

My phone rang. I look and it was Naomi calling.

"Hello?"

"Hey, Handsome."

"Hey, Beautiful. What's up?"

"Nothing really. I wanted to know if you're down to go to Scooters."

"I'm down. I've been there before. I'll pick you up after I run errands. I should be done at 2pm. Wear something nice for me."

"Ok," she said in the cutest voice.

Scooters Roller Palace reminded me of the movies *Roll Bounce* and *ATL*. My parents used to take me and Jafari there when we were younger.

I got regular rollerblades while Naomi got the skates on four wheels. We skated for two hours with breaks in between. It was a nice little getaway from all the drama that was going on in the family lately. It's even better to escape with a beauty like Naomi.

"So. Are you enjoying yourself?" I asked.

"Yup," she responded, sounding a little distant.

"What's up?" I asked, curious.

"Nothing. Everything is good. Why do you ask?"

"You don't see all there." I am in tune enough with her to know when something is off.

She was hesitant. "I have something to tell you."

"What's that?"

"I knew about your Mom's fraud before she got charged and taken into custody."

I was intrigued. "How?"

"Because I was supposed to do it with her."

"Why would you even consider it?"

"I had this debt that I wanted to clear up."

"Do you know why Mom did it?"

"Yes. She was stressing out about not having enough funds to pay bills while your Dad was recovering. She also said her savings was depleted quicker than she anticipated. I opted out because I thought it was risky. I don't know too much about how the fraud took place but I know it involved an account takeover and this guy name Oliver was in charge of coordinating it. An account takeover is when you gain control of an account and make unauthorized transactions. I was told Mom got caught because she committed the crime from a computer at the hospital, logged in with her staff information. All this talk about getting told on isn't true. She ratted herself out. The account she did the fraud on was being monitored. The police traced the unauthorized transactions back to the hospital's IP address. They did more of an investigation and traced it back to the computer your Mom logged into. She was told to never, *never* use a computer that could trace her login information. Only use Wifi with a Guest login. I guess she had her reasons for breaking the rules. Maybe she wasn't thinking straight."

"How long do you think she's going to get?"

"Man. This is federal. I think it's a minimum five years."

"Damn." I didn't know what else to say. "You know what I've been thinking about lately?"

"What's that?"

"I'm thinking about moving out. I'm going to see if I can get some sort of business plan going so I can be my own boss. I'm not working for anyone. I'm giving myself two years. I'll be twenty then."

"Mmm. Sounds like a plan."

Chapter 6

"I have something to tell you." Jafari said, sounding down.

"What's going on?" I asked.

"Dad has a new girlfriend." I couldn't believe my ears. The New Year is already at a rocky start.

"Are you sure *Dad* has a new girlfriend?"

"I haven't been so sure in all my life," he said with such confidence.

I was finally able to get one on one time with Dad. I wasted no time initiating the conversation. "Why?"

"Why what Isaiah?"

"Is it true?"

"Isaiah. What are you talking about?"

"You know *who* I am talking about!"

He paused. "Why don't you just tell me who you are referring to."

"Ms. Susie. Dad. Who is she?"

He paused again. "She's just a friend."

"Oh, yea?" I asked. "So, why do you have to go fly out so far to go see her if she's just a friend"

"I don't have to answer any of your questions. You're the son and I'm the father."

"It's not right Dad. Mom doesn't deserve this."

"Neither do I! Of all people, why was she committing fraud with *Oliver*? How would you feel if your wife was engaging in illegal activity with the very man she claimed made her uncomfortable? For all I know, she could have been sleeping with him too! What am I supposed to think?"

"Don't turn this around-"

"Answer the damn question, Isaiah!" Dad demanded, interrupting me.

"I wouldn't feel comfortable but-"

"No buts Isaiah-"

"No! Dad! Listen to me!" I demanded. "You don't have any proof that Mom did *anything* with this guy. All I'm saying is you shouldn't be stepping out on Mom like that without getting your facts straight. This is confusing. I look up to you but when I heard you've been with Ms. Susie, I now see you in a different light. And you shouldn't be encouraging Jafari to hold secrets like that for you. What are you teaching him?"

Dad didn't say a word. I was surprised because I thought he was going to knock me out but I didn't care. I had to speak my mind. Plus, what kind of son would I be if I didn't at least give Mom the benefit of the doubt? No one's perfect. It's a cliche hearing that statement but Dad's messing up. Ever since he got stabbed, he hasn't been the same. I pray he finds his balance again.

I called Haze.

"Hey man. What's up? Long time!" he said, sounding thrilled to hear my voice.

"We're moving to Mississauga."

"For real?"

"Yup. Time for a change. You know?"

"Yea. When are you moving?"

"The first week of February if everything goes through."

"Alright. Well, my parents will be gone for the weekend and I was thinking of throwing a little get-together. We can celebrate your last days in Scarborough."

"I'm cool with that. I'll call you when I get ready"

"Alright. Later."

Friday night came and I saw some familiar faces in the front of the house. It was more like a party and less of a "little" get-together. I parked at the plaza across the street because there was no parking available in front of the house. After parking, I headed on over and music was bumping.

Sean Paul's, "Get Busy" was playing. I didn't see Haze yet. He's probably upstairs with Renee or something. The party had an old-school, '90's vibe to it. I needed to take a leak, so I went to the bathroom. I washed my hands after finishing up. I came out and met Renee sanding by the washroom door as if she was waiting for me."

"Isaiah. Right?" She asked, even though I knew she already knew my name.

"Yea," I responded, defensively.

"You're looking nice." Her eyes seductively scanned my body.

"Thanks," I responded. Nonchalant.

"We should hang out sometime." I nodded my head thinking to myself, 'This girl is too bold.' "Give me your number and let's get to know each other."

"No. Haze is my friend and-"

"I like you though. My pussy is wet," she interrupted.

My dick got hard. The bulge was noticeable. She saw it, twirled her hair around and winked at me. As much as I was trying to resist her, she came on stronger.

She took her iPhone and punched in the number as I told her, 647...when Haze appeared at the door. He looked at her.

"What's up? Trying to take my woman?" He asked, jokingly.

"Hold up. She asked me-"

Haze interrupted "Yea. Ok!" He walked over to Renee.

"I didn't ask him for anything. Come, let me give you a kiss." Renee said to Haze, pulling him in to give him affection. As she hugged him with his face in the opposite direction, she looked at me for the last four digits. I mouthed 5077. Still, in his arms, she mouthed, "I'll call you."

A little over an hour went by and Renee came out of nowhere. She spotted me on the wall, posted up, minding my own business. The DJ threw on Kevin Lytle's, "Turn Me On." Everyone was catching a bubble. Renee danced up on me while I put my hands around her waist and pulled her in closer to me. She was peanut butter and I was jelly.

Her skin felt so soft. She rubbed her hands sensually around my body like I was the only man in the world.

The DJ changed the tune and Renee whispered, "Nice dance." I smiled and watched her walk away as she into the crowd.

I finally spotted Haze. He was dancing with some random girl, intertwined like origami.

Suddenly, I see a whole bunch of men coming from outside, dressed all in blue, infesting the crowd with their presence.

I went to strip Haze off of the lady he was dancing with. "Something's about to happen," I cautioned him. The men that came in started yelling, "C's up!"

Before we left the house, a fight broke out. Stampede was the next thing that happened while everyone tried to leave the house at the same time.

The police were there in no time. Haze and I, despite the cold, ran off like the Road Runner.

Chapter 7

The following week, I went to visit Mom. I didn't know how I was going to tell her about Dad's affair. I didn't even know if it was my place to say anything.

On my way there, I couldn't help but wonder how long I could keep Dad's affair from her. I felt torn.

The guard told me to have a seat and went to go get Mom. He returned and told me she doesn't want to see anyone today.

"Are you sure? Tell her Isaiah was here to see her."

"I did. A prisoner can refuse visits at their discretion."

I started to wonder why Mom was refusing visitors. The guard suggested I write down my name and address in hopes she will write back. I did just that and at the bottom of the page, I asked her to call. I wanted to hear her voice.

"There's mail for you on your bed," Dad said, bitterly.

I ripped open the envelope and read the following:

Dear Isaiah,

Sorry I couldn't see you the last time you came to visit. I needed to just meditate on some things. Don't stress over me, God's grace is holding me up. I hope the family is staying strong. Say hi to Naomi for me.

Love,
Mom

Two weeks went by and I was determined to see her again.

"Who are you here to visit?" A different guard asked. I told him my mom. "She's in solitary confinement and not allowed visitors for the rest of the week."

"Why?" I asked, baffled.

"She started a fight with another inmate."

"Damn," I said to myself. "I guess I'll come by when I'm able to see her."

Man, prison life must be rough for women as well as men. There's no fury like a woman scorned. I never heard of Mom getting into a fight. She was probably defending herself. I don't see her starting anything with anyone. Regardless, I hope she won. Just saying.

Chapter 8

This man has the nerve and I didn't see it coming. I was on my way back to go see Naomi and it was the last day of March break.

"Give me all of your money!" he whispered as he pushed me up against the wall at gunpoint. He had on a face mask. I couldn't recognize him.

I wasn't going down without a fight. I did what any real man would do and defended myself. I managed to get him in a headlock but he was strong enough to push me into the car. "You think you're all that. Eh?" I didn't understand why he was saying that. Must be jealousy or something. The gun dropped. It was either me or him. He went after the gun. I went after him. I speared him from behind to prevent him from getting the gun. I was contemplating whether or not I should kill him. Before I did anything, I took off his face mask. He didn't look familiar. I shot him in the leg just for trying to ambush me.

Not too long after, police arrived. Probably a scared pedestrian saw what happened and reported it from afar. Who knows.

I got sentenced to a year in jail for aggravated assault. If I didn't shoot him in the leg, I would get less time.

What made things worse is finding out that Dad passed away two months later. He was murdered by Susie. She ended up killing herself.

The only person I would let come visit me was Naomi. I didn't want Jafari to see me behind bars in a jumpsuit. I'm thankful that Grandma looked after Jafari after Dad passed away. He stayed with Grandma until Mom came out. I'm not a fan of Children's aid.

Mom was going to be released in four months. Her good behaviour reduced her time to be served in half. She was originally supposed to serve 2 years.

Before getting charged, I received letters from Mom, encouraging me to stay strong and look out for Jafari.

I was surprised when she told me about beating up a woman in jail. She also told me that she was excited to be getting out of prison.

Although I was spending time, I was able to attend Dad's funeral. His graveyard was located at the Derry West Cemetery in Mississauga. I took one last look at the casket before they closed it.

Naomi was right by my side. I couldn't help but think how Dad's violent death, Mom's absence as well as my own was going to affect Jafari. I know I was only going to be gone for a year but that's still a significant amount of time to be away from him. I taught him well. I just hope he applied what he learned now that I wasn't around. Hopefully.